Chita's
Christmas
Tree

by Elizabeth Fitzgerald Howard

illustrated by Floyd Cooper

Aladdin Paperbacks

First Aladdin Paperbacks edition 1993

Aladdin Paperbacks
An imprint of Simon & Schuster Children's Publishing Division
1230 Avenue of the Americas
New York, NY 10020

Printed in Hong Kong by South China Printing Company (1988) Ltd.
10   9   8   7   6   5   4   3   2
The text of this book is set in Tiffany Medium.
The illustrations are oil wash on board and mixed media reproduced in full color.
Typography by Julie Quan.
A hardcover edition of Chita's Christmas Tree *is available from*
Simon & Schuster Books for Young Readers.

Library of Congress Cataloging-in-Publication Data
Howard, Elizabeth Fitzgerald.
    Chita's Christmas tree / by Elizabeth Fitzgerald Howard; illustrated by
  Floyd Cooper.—1st Aladdin Books ed.
        p.   cm.
    Summary: Papa and Chita leave downtown Baltimore in a buggy to find a
  Christmas tree in the deep woods.
    ISBN 0-689-71739-3
    [1. Christmas tree—Fiction.   2. Christmas—Fiction.   3. Baltimore (Md.)—
  Fiction.   4. Afro-Americans—Fiction.]   I. Cooper, Floyd, ill.   II. Title.
  [PZ7.H83273Ch   1993]
  [E]—dc20   92-44482

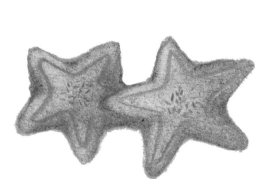

*For my cousin Chita
and for my daughters,
Jane, Susan, and Laura,
with love*

—E.F.H.

*For Lori
—F.C.*

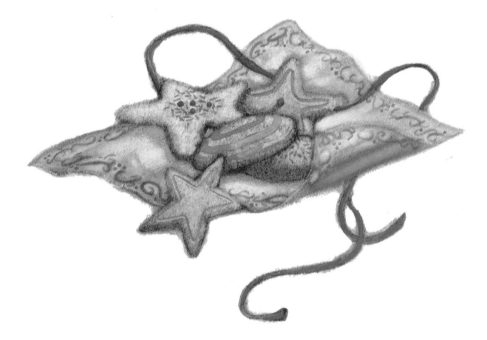

🌿 A SPECIAL SATURDAY

It is the Saturday before Christmas.
In a tall brick house in the middle of old Baltimore,
a little girl named Chita bounces out of bed.
"Mama!" Chita calls. "Mama! Is today the day?"
"Yes," says Mama. "Dress quickly and eat your oatmeal.
Papa is almost ready.
And Henry is stomping his feet."
"Will Papa listen to any hearts today?" asks Chita.
"No hearts, no pulses," says Papa. "My patients don't need
to see me today. Today we will ride into
the deep deep woods and find Chita's Christmas tree.
And then," Papa teases, "maybe Santa Claus will bring the tree
on Christmas Eve when Chita is sleeping."
Oh, Chita hopes!

Henry the horse is waiting for Chita and Papa,
just like every Saturday.
Chita always rides with Papa when he calls on his sick patients.
Mama has packed a snack, just like every Saturday.
Three peanut butter sandwiches.
Two for Papa, one for Chita.
But who wants a peanut butter sandwich when the waffle man
will be selling hot sugary waffles?
Henry does! He loves peanut butter.
"Bye, bye, Mama. Thank you for the sandwiches!"

Chita and Papa drive off with Henry.
Down Druid Hill Avenue.
Past Uncle Will's house. Past Uncle Bill's house.
Past the George Washington Monument
and the downtown shops all red and green for Christmas.

THE WAFFLE MAN

"Papa, there he is. The waffle man!"

"Ah, the waffle man!"

The waffle man waves to Chita and Papa.

"Good morning, waffle man," says Chita.

"Today Papa and I are going to find my Christmas tree,
and then Santa Claus will bring it to me."

The waffle man tweaks Chita's nose.

Delicious waffles!

Crispy and buttery, cinnamony and crunchy.

"Here, Henry. Here's your favorite snack!"

Delicious peanut butter sandwiches!

"Do you think we should tell Mama?" Chita always asks.

"We'll tell her next Saturday," Papa always answers.

"Oh no, Papa. This is our secret!"

And Henry is almost smiling.

🌿 THE DEEP DEEP WOODS

Now they drive a long long way, and leave the city.

It's frosty cold, but Chita and Papa are cozy and toasty,
tucked under the big buggy blanket.

"Maybe it will snow," says Papa.

"Maybe it will snow and snow and snow and snow!" shouts Chita.

Henry pulls the buggy into the deep deep woods.

Soon they come to where the pines and firs make
a green place in the gray-brown forest.
"Whoa, Henry," says Papa.
"Oh, Papa. So many Christmas trees!"
Chita walks around slowly, this way, that way.
But this tree is too scraggly.
And this one is too plump.
And this one is too stumpy.
And this one . . .
"Chita, Chita," teases Papa.
"My toes are nippy. My nose is drippy.
Which one will it be?"

"Oh, Papa. Look. Here it is! Here it is!"
Chita jumps up and down. This tree must be
the loveliest tree in the deep deep woods. The tallest,
the most graceful, its branches full and spreading.
"Oh, Papa! Its top almost scrapes the sky!"
"Good choice," says Papa.
Then he takes out his gold pocket knife.
Carefully he carves letters on the trunk of the tree:
C H I T A
They climb back into the buggy. Henry starts toward home.
"Do you think Santa Claus will bring the right tree?" asks Chita.
"Of course he will," says Papa.
"Because I have carved your name on it."
And Chita hugs Papa, tight.

BAKING COOKIES

It is Christmas cookie baking day at Chita's house.
Mama and Chita are wearing starchy white aprons.
Chita tries to stir the stiff dough
in the big cookie-dough bowl.
It is hard work. Mama has to help.
There is flour everywhere.
There is sugar on the floor.
And butter in Chita's hair.
More cookies.
More cookies.
Mama has the rolling pin.
"Let's cut out these cookies now, Chita," says Mama.
"Let me help you flatten down the dough."
"Mama, I can do it, I can do it."
Chita has dough on her ears and elbows.
On her cheeks. On her chin.

"I am making one for Papa.
A round cookie face with a raisin mustache!
I want to make some cookies for Santa Claus, too.
When he brings my tree. . .
Do you think he will bring the right tree, Mama?"
Mama smiles. "Didn't Papa put your name on the tree?"
"Yes, Mama, but I hope Santa Claus knows."
More cookies.
More cookies.
When they are finished, there are
twenty dozen sugar cookies shaped like stars.
And one round cookie face with a raisin mustache.
Made by Mama and Chita.
For Christmas.

CHRISTMAS EVE

It is Christmas Eve.
The aunts and uncles and cousins come for supper.
Everyone is all dressed up and fancy.
Uncle Bill and Uncle Will. Aunt Grace and Aunt Lucille.
Uncle Fitz has a red cravat.
Aunt Gert looks pretty in her Spanish shawl.
Cousin Mac's shoes are shiny,
Cousin May's dress is green.
Baby Cousin Jessie wears her gold heart locket.
Quiet, quiet while Papa reads the Christmas story.
Now. Supper!
There are creamed oysters. Smithfield ham.
Roasted chestnuts. Hominy. Sauerkraut.
Candied sweet potatoes.
Aunt Grace has brought her prize plum pudding.
And later, Chita and Mama march in with
big platters piled high.
Twenty dozen sugar cookies shaped like stars!
And one round cookie face with a raisin mustache.

After supper Mama sits down at the player piano.
"May I have this dance?"
Papa dances with Chita.
Cousin Mac dances with Cousin May.
Uncle Fitz swings Aunt Gert in a circle.

And outside the snow starts to fall.
It falls on Druid Hill Avenue.
On Uncle Will's house. On Uncle Bill's house.
It falls on the horses waiting patiently
to take the aunts and uncles and cousins home.
Coats, hats, muffs, mittens!
"Good-night, everyone! Good-night! Merry Christmas!"

Papa helps Chita hang one of his big woolly socks by the fireplace.
"Papa, do you think Santa Claus will really bring the right tree?"
"Yes," says Papa. "Because I carved your name on it.
And Santa Claus remembers everything."
Papa smiles at Mama.
Good-night hugs.
"Good-night, Papa. Good-night, Mama."

CHRISTMAS MORNING

Bong.
Bong.
Bong.
Bong.
Bong.
Bong.
Bong.

Bong. The grandfather clock is striking Christmas morning!
Chita wakes up. She tosses off her quilt
and bounces out of bed.
She races down the stairs and
runs to fling open the French doors to the living room.
She doesn't see Papa's woolly sock stuffed with lumpy things.
She doesn't see the picture book
or the doll with the smiling face.

But there . . .
its top touching the ceiling,
twinkling, sparkling,
its branches bright with shining balls . . .
Is it?
Chita has to push in close to be sure,
careful, careful not to break . . .
and there on the trunk,
she can read the letters:
C H I T A
Chita's Christmas tree!

"Merry Christmas, Mama and Papa!"
"Merry Christmas, Chita!"